For everyone at Little Tiger,
friends and family . . .
A very BIG thank you - J. L.

tiger tales
5 River Road, Suite 128,
Wilton, CT 06897
Published in the United States 2016
Originally published in Great Britain 2016
by Little Tiger Press
Text and illustrations copyright © 2016 Jonny Lambert
ISBN-13: 978-1-68010-032-7
ISBN-10: 1-68010-032-7
Printed in China
LTP//1400/1432/0216

For more insight and activities,
visit us at www.tigertalesbooks.com

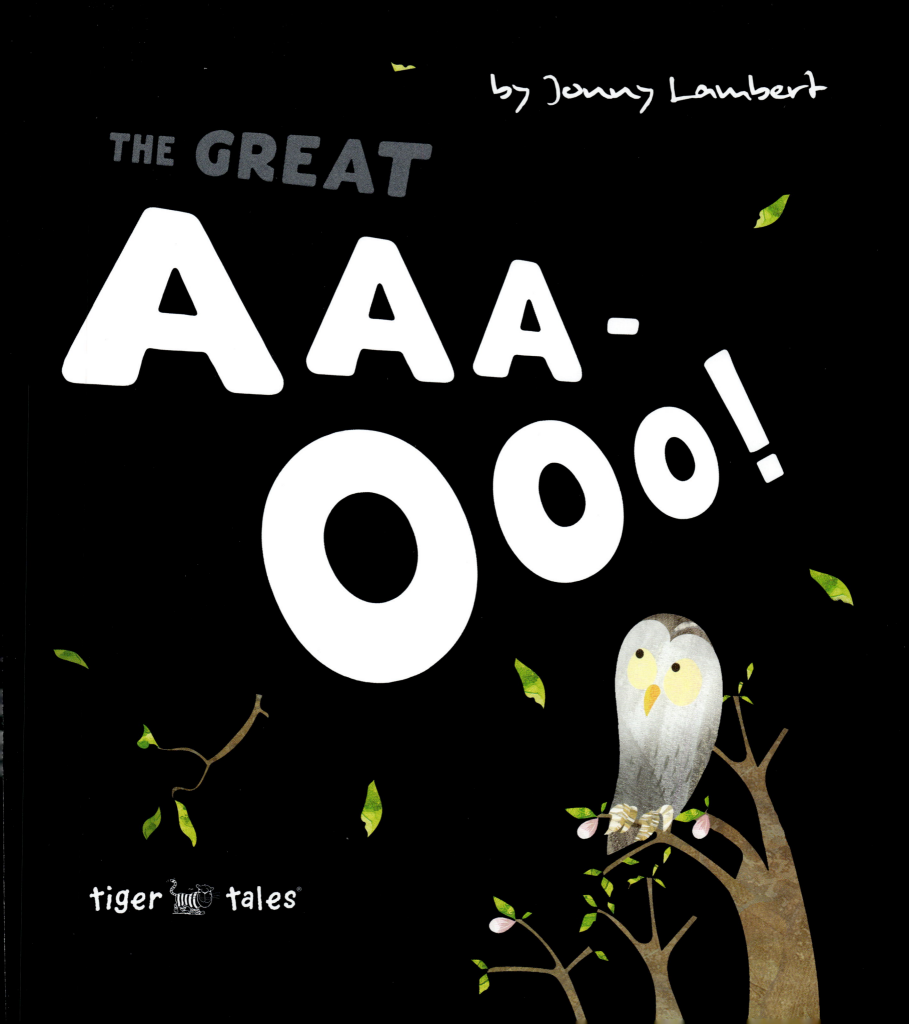

As Mouse scampered home through the dark woods, he heard a horrible howl.

AAA-Ooo!

Owl winked one beady eye.
"Hoo-hoo, was that you?"

"Not I," squeaked Mouse nervously.
"I...I...I thought it was you!"

"Not I!" hooted Owl. "If it was not you,
then who, hoo-hoo, is making this
awful AAₐ-Oₒₒ?"

AAA

Bear grumbled up the tree, disturbed from his slumber by the hullabaloo.
"Grrr!" he grizzled. "Which one of you made that awful AA$_A$-O$_O$O?"

"Not I!" Owl huffed. "I hoot and hoot hoo-hoo-hoo."

"Not I!" squeaked Mouse. "I scritch and scratch, squeak and chew, but never, ever do I AA$_A$-O$_O$O!"

A A

KNOCK, SMACK, THWACK, Moose banged
on the tree. "Hey, you up there . . .
yes, you . . . you three! Are you making
that horrible howl?"

"Not us," grunted Bear. "We growl, squeak, and hoo-hoo, but never, ever do we AA$_A$-O$_O$o!"

"Then WHO?" bellowed Moose. "WHO?"
Closer and closer came the awful . . .

A$_{AA}$-O$_O$o!

AA$_A$-O$_O$o!

AA$_A$-O$_O$o!

"It might be a monster," squeaked
   Mouse, "bug-eyed and blue . . . ."
"Or hairy and scary," cried Moose,
"with big claws—"
"And huge teeth,"
   added Bear, "that chomp,
   gnash, and chew!"

"Oh, what a mess!" hooted Owl.
"A monster in our woods?
   This will not do!"

AAA-OOO! AAA-OOO!

"It's a monster, all right! What will we do?"
cried Moose, as Duck, Goose, and Dove landed
with a startled QUACK, HONK, and COO!

"Quick! Get up here!" growled Bear,
scooping Wolf Cub from the ground.
"Something scary is coming, and it's
making a horrible sound!"

"Do monsters eat cubs?"
whimpered Wolf.

"Monsters eat everything!"
said Duck with a cry.

"We'll be plucked, stuffed,
and roasted, and put in a pie!"

"A pie?" roared Bear.

**"Save yourselves!
Follow me!"**

And the animals scrambled and
clambered higher into the tree.

TWIST!

BOUNCE!

BEND!

Branches BUCKLED!

The tree CREAKED, SHUDDERED,
and GROANED, then . . .

HONK!

BELLOW!

HOOT!

COO!

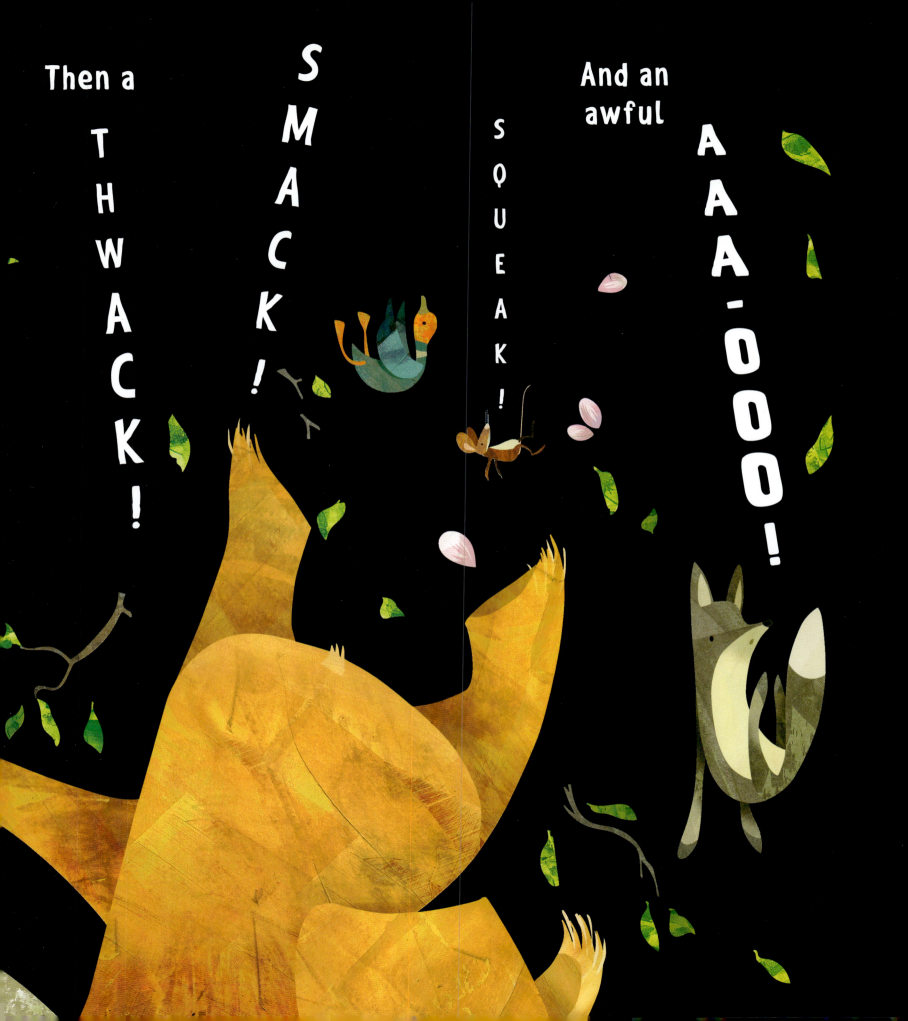

Then a
THWACK!

SMACK!

And an awful
AAA-OOO!

SQUEAK!

"WOLF!

It was you!" hooted Owl.
"You who made that horrible howl!"

"I'm sorry," whined Wolf.
"I didn't mean to give you
a fright. But when I'm alone
in the dark, lonely woods,
it's really SCARY at night."

Bear gave Wolf Cub a **huge** hug.

"There, there . . . it's all right.
If you promise to be quiet,
you can sleep with us tonight."

At long last, the noisy woods were peaceful once
more. The animals drifted off to sleep with a . . .

SNUFFLE, WHEEZE, SNORE . . .
SPUTTER, MUTTER, GRUMBLE, COO,
MUMBLE, MURMUR . . .

cock-a-d